13-Digit ISBN: 978-1-64643-018-5
10-Digit ISBN: 1-64643-018-2

This book may be ordered by mail from the publisher.
Please include $5.99 for postage and handling.
Please support your local bookseller first!

Books published by Cider Mill Press Book Publishers are available at special discounts for bulk purchases in the United States
by corporations, institutions, and other organizations. For more information, please contact the publisher.

Applesauce Press is an imprint of
Cider Mill Press Book Publishers
"Where good books are ready for press"
PO Box 454
12 Spring Street
Kennebunkport, Maine 04046
Visit us online! cidermillpress.com

Typography: Bembo Std and ITC Caslon

Printed in China
1 2 3 4 5 6 7 8 9 0
First Edition

THE Camel's Lament

A Lively Rhyming Ode to Animals

by Charles Edward Carryl ✳ Illustrated by Charles Santore

APPLESAUCE PRESS

KENNEBUNKPORT, MAINE

Canary birds feed on sugar and seed,

parrots have crackers to crunch;

and as for the poodles,
they tell me the doodles have chicken
and cream for their lunch.

But there's never a question about my digestion—
anything does for me!

Cats, you're aware,
can repose in a chair,

chickens

can roost upon rails;

puppies are able to sleep in a stable,

and **oysters**
can slumber in pails.

But no one supposes a poor camel dozes—
anyplace does for me!

Lambs are enclosed where it's never exposed,

coops are
constructed for hens;

kittens are treated to houses well heated,

and pigs are protected by pens.

But a **camel** comes handy wherever it's sandy—
anywhere does for **me!**

People would laugh if you rode a
giraffe  or mounted the
back of an OX;

it's nobody's habit
to ride on a rabbit

or try to bestraddle a
fox.

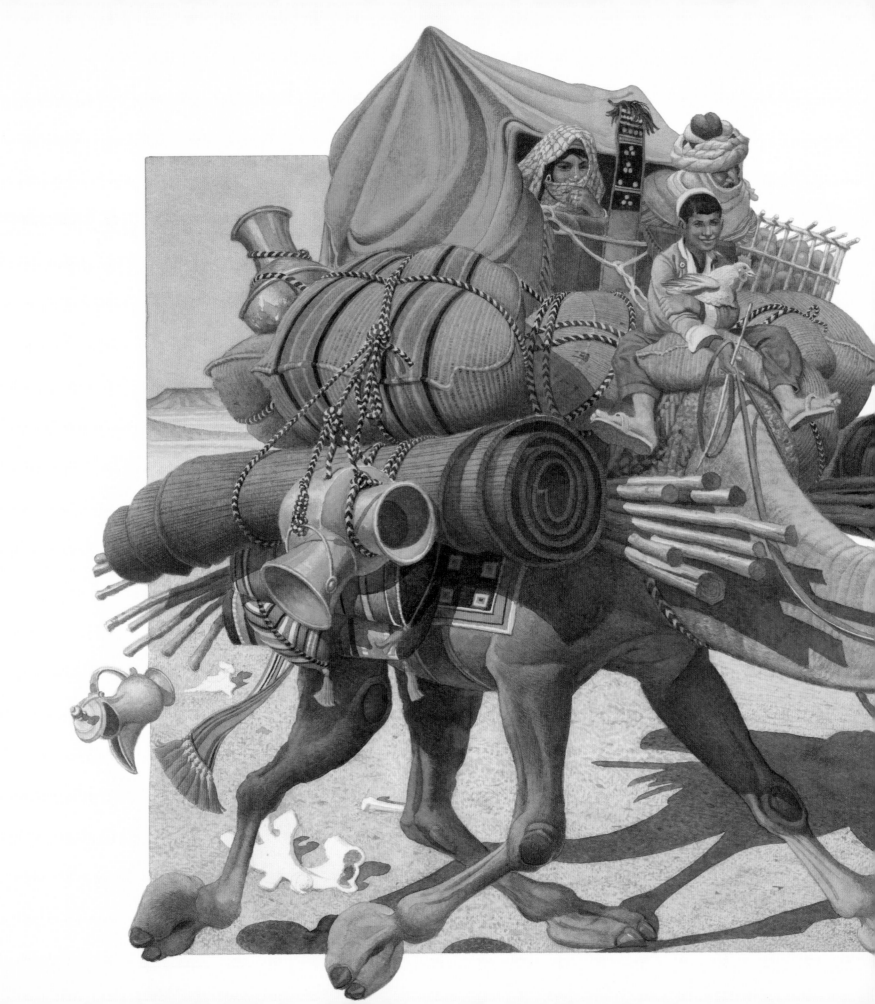

24

But as for a camel, he's ridden by families—
any load does for me!

A **snake** is as round

as a hole in the ground,

and

weasels

are wavy and sleek;

and no **alligator** could ever be straighter

than **lizards** that live in a creek.

But a camel's all lumpy and bumpy and humpy—
Any shape does for me!